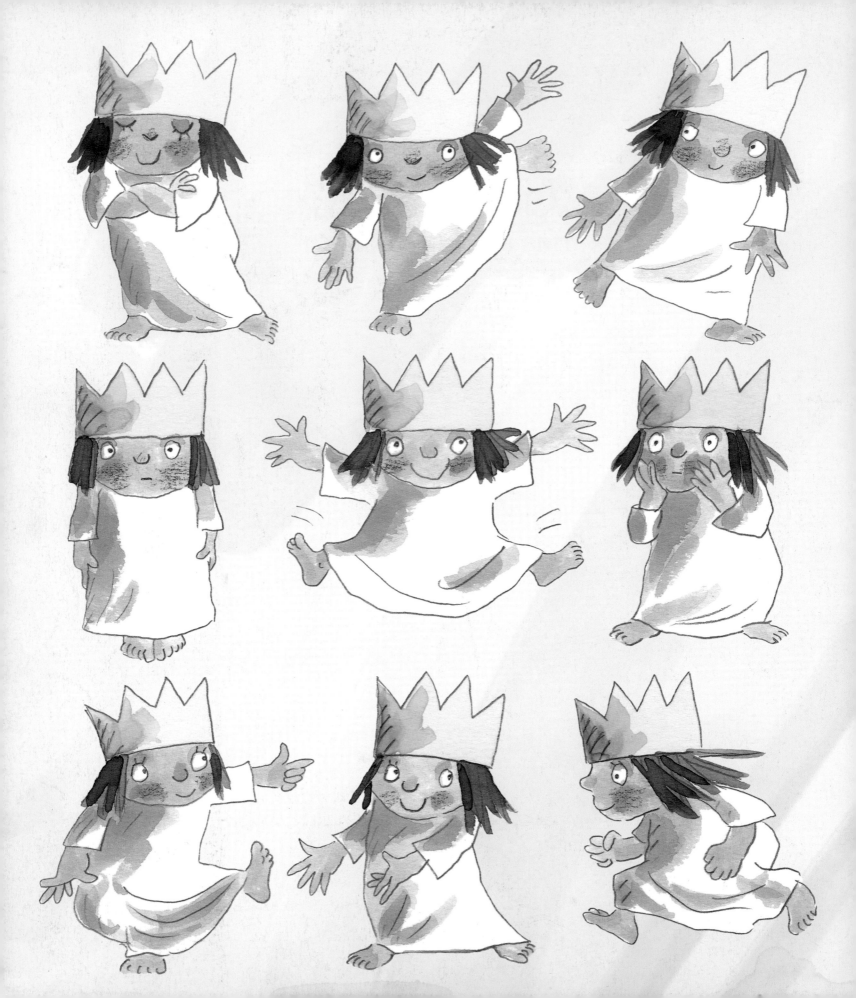

This paperback edition first published in 2017 by Andersen Press Ltd.

First published in Great Britain in 2003 by by Andersen Press Ltd.,

20 Vauxhall Bridge Road, London SW1V 2SA.

Copyright © 2003 by Tony Ross.

Printed and bound in Malaysia.

1   3   5   7   9   10   8   6   4   2

British Library Cataloguing in Publication Data available.

ISBN 978 1 78344 582 0

Little Princess

I Don't Want to Go to Bed!

Tony Ross

Andersen Press

"Why do I have to go to bed when I'm not tired, and get up when I am?" said the Little Princess.

"I don't WANT to go to bed!" she said.

"Bed is good for you," said the Doctor,
taking her upstairs. "Sleep is even better."

But the Little Princess came straight down again.
"I DON'T WANT TO GO TO BED!" she said.

"I WANT A GLASS OF WATER!"

"There you are," said the Queen.
"Sleepy, sleepy tighty."

"DAAAAAD!"

"You don't want another glass of water?" said the King.
"No," said the Little Princess. "Gilbert does."

"Nighty, nighty," said the King. "Sleepy tighty, Gilbert."
"Don't go!" said the Little Princess. "There's a monster
in the wardrobe."

"There's no such thing as monsters, and there are none in the wardrobe," said the King, closing the bedroom door.

"Dad!" shouted the Little Princess.
"What is it now?" said the King. "You're not
still frightened of monsters?"

"Of course I'm not," said the Little Princess. "Gilbert is.
He says there's one under the bed."

"No there isn't," said the King, creeping out of the bedroom.
"There's no such thing."

"Stop her!" shouted the Queen. "She's escaped."
"I DON'T WANT TO GO TO BED!" said the Little Princess.
"Why?" said the Queen.

"There's a spider over my bed...
and it's got hairy legs."

"Daddy's got hairy legs, and he's nice," said the Queen.

At last, the Little Princess went to bed.

Later, when the King went in to kiss her
goodnight, her bed was empty.

Everybody hunted high...

and low, until...

"Here she is," said the Maid. "She's keeping Gilbert and the cat safe from spiders and monsters."

The next morning, the Little Princess got up and
yawned a yawn. "I'm tired," she said...

"I want to go to bed."

My World of Science

BENDY AND RIGID

Angela Royston

www.heinemann.co.uk/library
Visit our website to find out more information about **Heinemann Library** books.

To order:
☎ Phone 44 (0) 1865 888066
▤ Send a fax to 44 (0) 1865 314091
▢ Visit the Heinemann Bookshop at www.heinemann.co.uk/library to browse our catalogue and order online.

First published in Great Britain by Heinemann Library, Halley Court, Jordan Hill, Oxford OX2 8EJ, part of Harcourt Education.

Heinemann is a registered trademark of Harcourt Education Ltd.

Editorial: Andrew Farrow and Dan Nunn
Design: Jo Hinton-Malivoire and
     Tinstar Design Limited (www.tinstar.co.uk)
Picture Research: Maria Joannou and Sally Smith
Production: Viv Hichens

Originated by Blenheim Colour Ltd
Printed and bound in China by
     South China Printing Company

ISBN 0 431 13728 5 (hardback)
07 06 05 04 03
10 9 8 7 6 5 4 3 2 1

ISBN 0 431 13734 X (paperback)
08 07 06 05 04
10 9 8 7 6 5 4 3 2 1

British Library Cataloguing in Publication Data
Royston, Angela
Bendy and rigid. – (My world of science)
1. Flexure – Juvenile literature
I. Title
620.1'1244

A full catalogue record for this book is available from the British Library.

Acknowledgements
The publishers would like to thank the following for permission to reproduce photographs:
Chris Honeywell p. **26**; David Bradford p. **24**; Eye Ubiquitous pp. **9**, **29** (Chris Fairclough); Getty Images pp. **20**, **25**; Photodisc p. **17**; Powerstock Zefa p. **12**; Rupert Horrox p. **8**; Trevor Clifford pp. **4**, **5**, **6**, **7**, **10**, **11**, **13**, **14**, **15**, **16**, **18**, **19**, **21**, **22**, **23**, **27**, **28**.

Cover photograph reproduced with permission of Trevor Clifford.

Every effort has been made to contact copyright holders of any material reproduced in this book. Any omissions will be rectified in subsequent printings if notice is given to the publishers.